Robin Hill School

The Playground Problem

For the real Emma—M. M.

First Aladdin Paperbacks edition April 2004

Text copyright © 2004 by Simon & Schuster, Inc.
Illustrations copyright © 2004 by Mike Gordon

ALADDIN PAPERBACKS
An imprint of Simon & Schuster Children's Publishing Division
1230 Avenue of the Americas
New York, NY 10020

Book design by Sammy Yuen Jr.
The text of this book was set in Century Schoolbook.

Manufactured in the United States of America
10

The Library of Congress Cataloging-in-Publication Data
McNamara, Margaret.
The playground problem / by Margaret McNamara ;
illustrated by Mike Gordon.—1st Aladdin Paperbacks ed.
p. cm.—(Robin Hill School)
Summary: When first-graders Nick, Jamie, and Reza refuse to let Emma join
their soccer game just because she is a girl, Emma and her father devise a
plan to teach the boys a lesson.
ISBN-13: 978-0-689-85876-5 (pbk.)
ISBN-10: 0-689-85876-0 (pbk.)
ISBN-13: 978-0-689-85877-2 (lib. bdg.)
ISBN-10: 0-689-85877-9 (lib. bdg.)
0510 LAK
[1. Sex role—Fiction. 2. Schools—Fiction. 3. Soccer—Fiction.]
I. Gordon, Mike, ill. II. Title.
PZ7.M47879343Pl 2004
[E]—dc21
2002155257

The Playground Problem

Written by Margaret McNamara
Illustrated by Mike Gordon

Ready-to-Read
Aladdin Paperbacks
New York   London   Toronto   Sydney   Singapore

Monday was a sunny day.

It was recess.
Mrs. Connor's first-grade
class was on
the playground.

The boys were playing soccer.
"Hey!" called Emma.
"May I play?"

"No," said Nick.

"No," said Jamie.

"No," said Reza.

"We do not want you
to play with us,"
said Nick.

"Why not?" asked Emma.
"Because you are a girl,"
said Reza. "And girls
do not play soccer."

Emma was mad.

Emma was
very mad.

Emma was
FURIOUS.

That night she told her dad
all about the boys.

He helped her
figure out a plan.

On Tuesday
the girls ran out
to the playground.

They had a soccer ball.

They played soccer.

"Hey!" said Reza.

"The girls can play soccer."

"They are pretty good,"
said Nick.

"They are very good,"
said Jamie. "Emma! Come
and join the boys' team."

"No," said Emma.
"I do not want to play
  on a team with just boys."

"Why not?" asked Nick.

"Figure it out," said Emma.

On Wednesday
it rained and rained.

The girls played
at the activity table.

The boys sat
and stared at the rain.

"What are they doing?"
asked Katie.
"They are figuring
it out," said Emma.

On Thursday
it was sunny again.
The girls were
scoring goals.

"Hey, Emma!" said Reza. "We figured it out."

"Boys and girls
can play together,"
said Jamie.

"They can play
on the same team,"
said Reza.

"We got it," said Nick.

From then on,
the boys and girls played
together.

Sometimes they played
really well together.

Sometimes they had fights.

"I figure that
playing together makes us
the best team
we can be," said Reza.

And he was right.